Holly
the Christmas
Fairy

For Holly Sarah Williams,
my beautiful niece

Special thanks to
Narinder Dhami

ISBN 978-0-439-92880-9

All rights reserved. Published by Scholastic Inc., 557 Broadway, New York, NY 10012, by arrangement with Rainbow Magic Limited.

14   13   12   11 12 13 14 15/0
Printed in the U.S.A.   40

This edition first printing, October 2007

Holly
the Christmas
Fairy

by Daisy Meadows

LITTLE APPLE

SCHOLASTIC INC.

New York   Toronto   London   Auckland
Sydney   Mexico City   New Delhi   Hong Kong

The Fairyland Palace

Hillfields Farm

Christmas Trees

HILLFIELDS FARM

Tippington Town

Santa's Missing Sleigh

Christmas plans may go awry,
If I can make these reindeer fly.
Santa's gifts for girls and boys,
Will all become my fun, new toys!

Magic reindeer listen well,
As I bind you with this spell.
Hear my orders, fly this sleigh,
Through starry skies and far away.

Find the hidden letters in holly leaves throughout the book. Unscramble all 9 letters to make a special holiday word!

Contents

A Magical Mistake

"Only three days to go!" Rachel Walker said, sighing happily. She was attaching Christmas cards to long pieces of red ribbon, so that she could hang them on the living room wall. "I love Christmas! Don't you, Kirsty?"

Kirsty Tate, Rachel's best friend, nodded. "Of course," she replied, handing Rachel another pile of cards. "It's a magical time of year!"

Rachel and Kirsty laughed, and touched the golden lockets they both

wore around their necks. The two girls shared a wonderful secret. No one else knew it, but they were friends with the fairies! Kirsty and Rachel had visited Fairyland several times when their fairy friends needed help. The first time, they had rescued the Rainbow Fairies after they were cast out of Fairyland by nasty Jack Frost. Then Jack Frost and his goblin servants had stolen the magical tail feathers from

Doodle, the rooster that controlled the
weather in Fairyland. The girls had
helped the Weather Fairies get all of
Doodle's feathers back.

In return, the Fairy King and Queen
had given Rachel and Kirsty each a gold
locket. The lockets were full
of magical fairy dust. The
girls could use it to take
them to Fairyland
whenever they needed
help from the fairies.

"Thanks for inviting
me to visit," said Kirsty,
cutting another piece of ribbon. "Mom
says she and Dad will pick me up on
Christmas Eve."

"We might get some snow before
then!" Rachel said, smiling. "The

weather's getting much colder. I wonder what Christmas is like in Fairyland."

Just then, the door opened and Mrs. Walker came into the room. She was followed by Buttons, Rachel's friendly, shaggy dog. He was white with gray patches and had a long, furry tail.

"Oh, girls, that looks great!" Rachel's mom exclaimed when she saw the cards hanging on the wall. "We'll go over to Hillfields Farm and pick out a Christmas tree tonight."

"Hooray!" Rachel cried. "Can Kirsty and I decorate it?"

"We were hoping you would!" Mrs. Walker laughed. "You can get the decorations out of the garage after lunch."

"Buttons seems to love Christmas, too," Kirsty said, smiling. The dog was sniffing around the cards and ribbons.

"He does," Rachel replied. "Every year, I buy him some doggie treats and wrap them up. And every year, he finds them and eats them before Christmas!"

Buttons wagged his tail. Then he

grabbed the end of a ribbon in his mouth and ran off, trailing red ribbon behind him.

"Buttons, no!" Rachel yelled. She and  Kirsty ran after him to get the ribbon back. When the girls had finished hanging the Christmas cards, they had some hot soup for lunch. Then Rachel took Kirsty out to the garage to find the boxes of decorations.

"It's getting colder," Kirsty said, shivering. "Maybe it will snow!"

"I hope so," Rachel replied. She switched on the garage light. "The decorations are up there." She pointed at a shelf above the workbench. "I'll stand on the stepladder and hand the boxes down to you."

"OK," Kirsty agreed.

Rachel climbed up the ladder and began to pass the boxes down. They were full of silver stars, shiny tinsel, and glittering balls in pink, purple, and silver.

"I hope you have a fairy for the top of the tree," Kirsty joked as Rachel handed her a box.

"No, we don't!" Rachel laughed. "We've always had a silver star, but it's getting old now. Be careful, Kirsty," she continued, lifting another box off the shelf. "This one has all sorts of things sticking out of it.

"Oh!" Rachel gasped in surprise. The gold locket around her neck had caught on a tiny, sparkling wreath made of twigs. The locket burst open, scattering both girls with fairy dust.

8

"Oh, no!" Rachel cried, scrambling down from the ladder.

"What should we do?" Kirsty asked.

But they didn't have time to do anything. Suddenly, both girls were caught up in a swirling cloud of fairy dust that swept them off their feet. The sparkles whirled around them, glittering in the pale winter light.

"Kirsty, we're shrinking!" Rachel cried. "I think we're on our way to Fairyland!"

Christmas Chaos

The girls weren't scared. This had happened to them before! But as they whirled through the clouds toward Fairyland, Rachel felt a little embarrassed. She hadn't meant to use her magic fairy dust at all — it was an accident!

"Don't worry," called Kirsty, noticing

the look on Rachel's face. "It will be great to see our fairy friends again."

Soon the girls spotted the red-and-white toadstool houses of Fairyland below, and then the silver palace with its four pink towers. As Rachel and Kirsty drifted closer to the palace, they could see a crowd of fairies waving at them. There was King Oberon and

Queen Titania with the
Rainbow Fairies and all
of the Weather
Fairies, too.
Even
Doodle, the
fairy rooster,
had come to
greet them.
"Hello!"
called Ruby
and Sunny.
"It's wonderful
to see you!" cried
Pearl and Storm.
As the girls landed on the
ground, the fairies crowded
around them.

Rachel quickly tried to explain. "I'm sorry," she gasped. "We didn't mean to come. It was an accident."

The queen smiled. "No, it wasn't an accident!" she said in her silvery voice. "Fairy magic made your locket open. I'm afraid we need your help again, girls!"

The two friends turned to look at each other in surprise, their eyes wide.

"Is it Jack Frost again?" Kirsty asked.

"We'll tell you all about it," replied the queen. "But first . . ." She waved her wand at Rachel's locket. It filled with fairy dust again and swung shut.

"Now," the king said, turning to the fairies. "Where is Holly the Christmas Fairy?"

Kirsty and Rachel watched eagerly as Holly came forward. They had never met the Christmas Fairy before! She had long dark hair, and wore a red dress that was exactly the same color as a holly berry. Her dress had a hood with fuzzy white trim. Even though Holly

was the Christmas Fairy, she looked
awfully sad.

"Holly is in charge of putting the
sparkle into Christmas," Queen Titania
explained.

"That's right," Holly said, sighing. "I
organize Santa's elves and I teach the
reindeer to fly. It's my job to make sure

that Christmas is as sparkly and happy as possible."

"But this year, Jack Frost is causing trouble," the king told them. "He had said he was sorry for everything he'd done and promised to behave."

"But now, he's up to his old tricks again," Queen Titania added.

"What happened?" Rachel asked.

"Well, Jack Frost sent a letter to Santa Claus asking for presents," the king revealed. "But he got a letter back! It said that he'd been so naughty, he wouldn't get any presents at all this year!"

"We'll show you what Jack Frost did next," said the queen. She waved her wand over a small pool of blue water on the ground. The water bubbled and fizzed, and then became smooth as glass.

Pictures appeared on the surface. Kirsty and Rachel could see a big log cabin at night. It was surrounded by deep snow,

and icicles hung from the wooden roof.
The cabin was full of toys! There were
dolls, puzzles, bikes, games, and books,
all lying around in huge piles. Kirsty and
Rachel had never seen so many toys.

"Oh!" Kirsty gasped. Her hand flew to
her mouth. "Rachel, look!"

In the corner of the cabin stood a
beautiful wooden rocking horse. Someone
was painting gold patterns onto the

rockers. He was dressed in red and white, and had a jolly face with a long white beard.

"It's Santa Claus!" Rachel cried happily.

Then the picture changed to show the outside of the cabin again. There, the girls could see Santa's sleigh. It was silver and white, and sparkled with magic. Eight reindeer were harnessed to the sleigh. They were all waiting patiently, shaking their antlers every so often.

Lots of little elves wearing bright green scurried around the sleigh, filling it with presents. The bells on the tips of their hats tinkled merrily as they rushed back and forth with armfuls of presents.

Kirsty and Rachel were so excited, they almost forgot why they were watching. But then, just as the sleigh was filled with presents, Jack Frost appeared.

As Kirsty and Rachel watched, Jack Frost peeked out from behind the log cabin. When the elves had left the sleigh, he ran over to it and jumped

in. Grabbing the reins, Jack Frost shouted a spell to make the reindeer obey him. And then, the sleigh lifted off the ground and zoomed off into the starry night sky.

As soon as the elves saw what was happening, they chased Jack Frost. But the magic sleigh was much too fast for them to catch.

"Oh, no!" Kirsty cried. "He stole Santa's sleigh!"

"So now you see why we need your help," said Queen Titania as the pictures faded away. "Holly has to find Santa's sleigh and return it before Christmas Eve. Otherwise, Christmas will be ruined for children around the world!"

"We think Jack Frost has taken the sleigh to your world," Holly added. "He loves parties, so he won't want to miss Christmas. Will you help me track him down?"

"Of course we will," Rachel and Kirsty replied together.

Holly smiled. "Thank you!" she cried, giving both girls a hug.

"Where should we start?" asked Rachel.

"Like usual, the magic will come to you," Queen Titania said with a smile. "You will know when you're on the right track. And Holly will

help. But there is just one more thing you
need to know. . . ." The queen waved
her wand over the pool again. The girls
watched as an image of three presents
appeared in the water. They were
wrapped in beautiful golden paper and
tied with big bows that glittered in every
color of the rainbow.

"These three presents were on the
sleigh when Jack Frost took it. They are
very special," the queen explained.
"Please try to find them all!"

"We'll do our best," said Kirsty, while
Rachel nodded.

The king stepped forward, holding a golden bag. "This will help you defeat Jack Frost," he said. He opened the bag and showed the girls a sparkling fairy crown. "It has

powerful magic. If Jack Frost puts this on his head, he will immediately be brought here, where he will appear before me and Queen Titania."

Kirsty took the bag and put the strap over her shoulder.

"Good luck, Rachel and Kirsty!" called the queen. She raised her wand and sent another shower of fairy dust whirling and swirling around the girls.

Buttons on the Loose!

"We're back!" Rachel said as the sparkling clouds of fairy dust cleared. The girls were in the Walkers' garage again.

"And we're back to normal size," Kirsty added, brushing a speck of fairy dust from her jeans. "Poor Holly. I hope we can help her."

"We'll find Jack Frost!" said Rachel. "But we'd better take these Christmas decorations inside now. Mom will wonder where we've been."

Kirsty dropped the tiny golden bag into her pocket for safekeeping. Then she helped Rachel carry the boxes into the house. Once the girls were inside, they started looking through the decorations.

"I see what you mean about this star," Kirsty said, holding up a big, tattered silver star.

"Maybe Mom will let me buy something new for the top of the tree," replied Rachel. "I'd love to have a fairy this year!"

The girls spent the rest of the afternoon sorting through the decorations. Rachel's dad got home from work at six o'clock, and then they all went to Hillfields Farm to pick out a Christmas tree.

"It looks like everyone else had the same idea!" Rachel's mom said as the car pulled up outside the farm. Lots of people were looking at Christmas trees.

There seemed to be hundreds of trees in all shapes and sizes.

"At least there are plenty of trees!" Kirsty laughed.

"And we'll find the perfect one," Rachel added, climbing out of the car.

The two girls hurried across the parking lot, and Mr. and Mrs. Walker followed with Buttons. The evening was cold and clear, and stars glittered in the dark sky.

"Don't pick one that's too big," called

Mrs. Walker. "We'll never get it through the front door."

Rachel and Kirsty wandered up and down the rows of trees. But they couldn't seem to find one that was just right. They were all too big, too small, too bushy, or too skinny.

Then Rachel's eyes fell on a tree up ahead. The needles were so green and shiny they almost seemed to glow in the frosty air. *That tree looks perfect*, she thought as she went over to it. *It's not too big and it's not too small.* Suddenly, Rachel spotted a bright red glow, right in the middle of the tree. Then a tiny face peeked out at her.

"It's me!" Holly cried, waving her wand and sending sparkly red holly berries bouncing around the tree branches.

Rachel laughed. "Kirsty, over here!" she called.

Kirsty rushed over. "What are you doing here, Holly?" she asked. "Is Jack Frost nearby?"

But before Holly could answer, there was a shout from Mrs. Walker. Buttons ran past the girls, his leash trailing along behind him. He was barking loudly.

"Stop him, girls!" cried Mrs. Walker. "I don't know what's wrong with him. He pulled the leash right out of my hand."

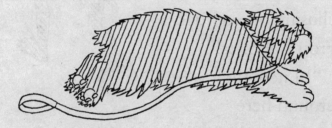

"We'll catch him, Mom," Rachel called. "Keep an eye on our tree."

Holly hopped inside Kirsty's pocket, and then the girls ran after the excited dog. Buttons had left the farmyard and was racing toward an oak tree.

Suddenly, Kirsty saw a shadow jump out from behind the tree and head for an old barn. Even though it was dark, she could just make out a pointed nose and big feet.

"Oh!" she gasped. "I think Buttons is chasing one of Jack Frost's goblins!"

"I knew they were around here somewhere!" Holly cried. "Quick! After him!"

Buttons was standing outside the barn, sniffing at the door.

"The goblin must be inside," Rachel whispered, grabbing the dog's leash. Quickly, she hooked it over a nail in the

barn wall, and gave Buttons
a pat. "Wait here,
Buttons," she
whispered. "We
won't be long."

"Let's look inside,"
Kirsty suggested. She pulled
the barn door open and they
all peeked in. A cold blast of icy air
swirled around them. The girls and Holly
could see across the barn to the big doors
on the opposite side. Those doors were
wide open, and a sparkling trail led out
of the barn and up into the sky. They
could just make out a glittering silver
shape traveling very fast. It was Santa's
missing sleigh!

Grumpy Goblins

"Jack Frost was here," Kirsty said, looking disappointed. "We just missed him!"

"That must be why it's so cold," Holly agreed with a shiver.

The barn was full of bales of straw. Looking around, Rachel noticed that there was wrapping paper scattered all over them. "Jack Frost has been opening

37

Santa's presents!" she said. "Isn't he awful?"

"Shh!" Holly whispered. "Goblins!"

Two goblins had just rolled out from behind one of the straw bales. They were fighting and yelling at each other.

"It's mine!" shouted one goblin with a wart on his nose.

"No, it's mine!" yelled the other.

"Look," Rachel said. She pointed at the present the goblins were arguing over. "It's one of the three special presents that the queen asked us to look for!"

"We have to get that present back," said Holly.

"The other two presents must still be on the sleigh," Kirsty added. "I don't see any more of that special gold wrapping paper anywhere."

The goblins were still fighting, rolling around on the floor of the barn.

"Give it to me!" yelled the warty one. "There might be Christmas cookies inside, or fruitcake, or —"

The other goblin licked his lips. "I'm going to eat them all!"

"What are we going to do?" Rachel whispered. "How are we going to get the present back?"

Kirsty frowned. "I have an idea," she said. "That goblin seems to like Christmas cookies. Holly, could you use your magic to make it smell like cookies?"

Holly's eyes twinkled. "Of course," she replied.

"We'll tell the goblins there's a big plate of cookies in the hayloft," Kirsty continued. "They're so greedy, they'll go and look. And they can't climb the ladder and hang on to the present at the same time. We'll be able to grab it!"

Rachel and Holly beamed at her.

"Great idea!" said Holly. "One magic Christmas cookie smell coming up!" She flew toward the goblins.

Holly's Magic Trick

Rachel and Kirsty watched anxiously as Holly fluttered over the goblins' heads. They were so busy fighting, they didn't even notice her.

Holly waved her wand in the air. A few seconds later, the smell of freshly baked cookies wafted around the barn.

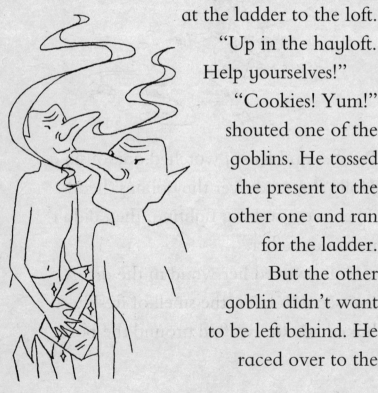

Even Rachel and Kirsty, who were standing outside, could smell it.

The goblins stopped fighting. They lifted their big noses into the air and sniffed.

"Fresh cookies!" Holly called, pointing at the ladder to the loft. "Up in the hayloft. Help yourselves!"

"Cookies! Yum!" shouted one of the goblins. He tossed the present to the other one and ran for the ladder. But the other goblin didn't want to be left behind. He raced over to the ladder, too. As soon as he realized that he couldn't climb up to the loft with the present in his arms, he threw it down on a pile of straw.

Rachel and Kirsty laughed as they watched the goblins scrambling up the ladder, trying to push each other out of the way. Once they had reached

the top, the girls dashed into the barn.
Kirsty picked up the present.

Suddenly, there was a shout from
above. "There aren't any cookies here!
We've been tricked!"

One of the goblins peered down into
the barn. "Where's that Christmas fairy?"
he yelled.

"Quick!" Holly gasped. "Let's get out
of here!"

The girls and Holly ran for the door as
the goblins tumbled
down the ladder.
"After them!" the
first goblin shouted.

Outside of the barn,
Rachel fumbled to
free Buttons's leash from
the nail. The goblins appeared in the
doorway and ran toward her. But Buttons
began to bark loudly as soon as he saw
them. The goblins looked frightened.

"*You* get the present back!" the first
goblin yelled, nudging the other.

"No, *you* get it!" his friend shouted.

Still barking, Buttons began pulling
Rachel toward the goblins. Immediately,
the two terrified goblins sprinted back
into the barn and shut the door.

47

"Good dog!" said Rachel, patting Buttons to calm him down. At the same time, Kirsty showed the present to Holly.

"Hooray! We've found one special present." Holly beamed. "I'll get this back to Fairyland right away." She waved her wand over the gift. The present disappeared in a magic cloud of sparkling red holly berries.

"We'll see you again soon," Rachel called as Holly fluttered up into the sky.

"I'll be back as soon as I find out where Jack Frost is!" Holly promised.

Rachel and Kirsty hurried back to the farmyard to find Mr. and Mrs. Walker. They had bought the tree Rachel had picked out and were tying it to the roof of the car.

"Now, I think it's time we all went home and had some Christmas cookies and hot chocolate," said Rachel's mom as they climbed into the car.

Rachel and Kirsty grinned at each other.

"Cookies would be great, Mom," said Rachel, trying not to laugh.

"I think Buttons deserves a cookie, too," Kirsty whispered. "After all, he was the one who led us to the goblins and the first present."

Woof! Buttons agreed.

"Yes, and our fairy adventures aren't over yet," Rachel whispered back, her eyes shining. "We'll save the sleigh. This is going to be the best Christmas ever!"

A Narrow
Escape

Contents

Christmas shopping

"Two days until Christmas!" Rachel said the next morning. She stood in front of the bedroom mirror, brushing her hair. The girls were getting ready to go Christmas shopping with Rachel's mom. "Isn't it exciting, Kirsty?"

Kirsty nodded. "I can't wait!" she said.

"But I don't want it to get here *too* soon.
We have to find Jack Frost and Santa's
sleigh first."

"I know," Rachel agreed. "Once we're
done helping our fairy friends, we can
really enjoy Christmas."

"I need to buy a present for my mom,"
Kirsty said. "Do you have many presents
left to buy?"

 Rachel shook her head.
"Only one," she replied.
"But the mall has great
Christmas displays, so
it's fun to look around
even if you don't have
much shopping to do."

"Girls, are you ready yet?" Mrs.
Walker called up the stairs.

"Coming, Mom!" Rachel yelled back.

The girls ran downstairs, laughing and chatting. Mrs. Walker was waiting for them in the hall. "Don't forget your scarves and mittens," she said, picking up her car keys. "It's freezing today, and the mall parking lot is big. We may have to walk a little after we park the car." She opened the front door and went to get the car out of the garage.

Rachel shivered as a blast of cold air swept through the open door. It rustled through the tinsel on the Christmas tree. "Brr!" she gasped, grabbing her coat. "Mom's right. It *is* cold today."

"Doesn't the tree look pretty?" asked

Kirsty, pulling on her mittens. The Walkers had a big entrance hall, and they had put the tree in a corner near the stairs. Rachel and Kirsty had decorated it, and now the tree glittered with balls, tinsel, and garland.

"It's the nicest one we've ever had,"

Rachel agreed. "But I'll unplug the lights now, since we're going out."

Kirsty watched as Rachel unplugged the Christmas tree lights. Then she noticed that something was different about the tree. Instead of the tattered silver star that she had placed on the top, there now sat a beautiful, sparkly fairy! Kirsty stared in surprise and realized that it was a *real* fairy. Holly was perched on top of the tree, glowing brightly and waving at Kirsty!

"Holly!" Kirsty laughed. "What are you doing up there?"

"I thought your tree was missing a fairy!" Holly grinned.

Rachel looked up in time to see Holly fly down and land on Kirsty's shoulder. "Hello, Rachel," Holly sang. "I have a feeling something magical is going to happen today! Can I come to the mall with you?"

"Of course," Rachel replied happily. "But you'll have to hide from my mom!"

"No problem," Holly winked at the girls and snuggled down inside Kirsty's coat pocket, folding her wings away neatly. She popped out a second later and said, "Don't forget the magic crown!"

"It's in my pocket," Rachel assured her.

Just then, they heard Rachel's mom honk the car horn.

"I hope something magical happens today!" Rachel whispered to Kirsty as they rushed outside. "Maybe we'll get Santa's sleigh and the two special presents back."

"I hope so!" Kirsty agreed with a smile.

Santa's Workshop

Even though it was still early in the morning, the mall was already crowded when they arrived. Mrs. Walker drove around the parking lot, and it took them a while to find an empty space.

"Now, Rachel," Mrs. Walker said as they all climbed out of the car, "would you and Kirsty like to go shopping on your own? I have to buy some presents that I don't want you to see!"

"Like what?" Rachel asked curiously.

Her mom laughed. "If I tell you, then they won't be a surprise, will they?" she said. "We'll split up, and I'll meet you and Kirsty in an hour by the glass elevators. Make sure you stay inside the mall, and stick together."

"OK," the girls agreed.

Mrs. Walker went up the elevator, while the girls stayed on the first floor. They walked around the mall, looking at Christmas displays in the store windows. Christmas songs were playing over the speaker system, and people were rushing all around, carrying lots of shopping bags.

Before long, Rachel and Kirsty had finished their Christmas shopping. Kirsty bought some pretty silver earrings for her mom, and Rachel bought a book for her dad.

"Are you OK in there, Holly?" Kirsty
whispered, putting the earrings into her
other pocket.

Holly nodded. She was peeking out of
Kirsty's pocket to
see what was going
on. She was so
small, nobody
noticed her amid
the hustle and bustle.

"Let's go see the Christmas display,"
Rachel said to Kirsty. "It's beautiful!"

Kirsty nodded eagerly, and Rachel led
the way to the big central area of the
mall. There, right in front of them, was
Santa's workshop.

"Wow!" said Kirsty, her eyes wide.
"This is fantastic!"

The workshop was a huge white tent

covered in sparkling lights. They changed color, from white to blue to silver, and then back again. Long, glittering icicles hung from the roof. The tent was surrounded by fake snow, and there were huge toy polar bears and penguins that waved at shoppers. Next to the tent, there was a small ice rink. Boys and girls dressed as elves were skating back and forth. Some carried brightly wrapped packages, while others performed spins and jumps.

A little bridge made of sparkling icicles led the way into the tent.

"Isn't it pretty?" Rachel asked as they moved closer to get a better look.

There was a long line of children waiting to see Santa. Rachel and Kirsty were standing near the bridge, watching the elves on the ice rink, when a little girl ran out of the tent to join her mom. She seemed upset! Kirsty and

Rachel couldn't help overhearing what
she said.

"Did you have a good time, honey?"
the mother asked.

"Well, Santa's sleigh was all sparkly,"
the little girl told her breathlessly,
"and the reindeer were furry
and friendly. But Santa
wasn't very nice!" She stuck
out her bottom lip as if she
was about to cry. "He
wouldn't give me a present,
even though he had lots and lots of them.
And he was all cold and spiky!"

Immediately, Rachel's ears pricked up.
That didn't sound like Santa at all. But it
did sound like someone else she
knew — someone mean and tricky. They
might have just found Jack Frost!

Not the Real Santa!

"Kirsty!" Rachel said, pulling her friend to one side. She didn't want their conversation to be overheard. "Did you and Holly hear that? I think Jack Frost might be inside the tent, pretending to be Santa!"

Kirsty stared at Rachel. "You could be right!" she gasped.

"Yes," Holly piped up. "We'd better check it out."

"How are we going to get into the tent?" asked Rachel. "It'll take forever if we have to wait in the line."

"She's right," Kirsty said. "Let's try to slip in the back and see what's going on."

The girls crept around the back of the tent, keeping an eye out for anyone who might try to stop them. But they found that the tent was tied down so firmly, they couldn't sneak underneath.

"Leave it to me!" Holly whispered. She waved her wand, and a shower of sparkling red fairy dust fell onto one corner of the tent. Immediately, the ropes loosened, and part of the canvas curled upward.

"Thanks, Holly!" said Rachel. "Come on, Kirsty."

The two girls crept cautiously under the edge of the tent. Inside, there were lots of glittering ice-covered rocks. Rachel, Kirsty, and Holly hid behind them while they looked around.

The tent was lit with rainbow-colored lanterns that glowed brightly. Long, gleaming icicles hung from the ceiling, and a big Christmas tree stood in one corner. It was decorated with shiny silver balls and multicolored fairy lights.

Kirsty shivered. The air inside the tent felt frosty. "It's really cold in here," she whispered. "Jack Frost must be nearby."

And, sure enough, in the middle of the room was Santa's sparkling sleigh, complete with hundreds of presents, eight magical reindeer, and Jack Frost! He was ripping open a package. The ground in front of him was already covered with wads of wrapping paper. He wore a red Santa suit and a fake white beard. But he still looked like his mean, cold self.

"Bring me another present!" he roared, tossing aside the game he'd just opened.

His goblin servants came rushing from every corner of the tent. They were all carrying presents, which they pushed into Jack Frost's greedy hands. Rachel and Kirsty held their breath nervously as the goblins hurried past their hiding place.

Suddenly, Kirsty spotted something. "Look!" she hissed, pointing at the sleigh. "It's one of the special presents!" The gold-wrapped package was sitting at the back of the sleigh, on top of a pile of other presents.

"You're right," Holly whispered excitedly. "And the third one must still be on the sleigh somewhere, too. It doesn't look like Jack Frost has opened it already."

"But how are we going to get them without Jack Frost and his goblins seeing us?" Rachel asked.

"If we stay behind the rocks, we can crawl around to the back of the sleigh without being seen," said Kirsty.

"And I can help you," Holly added eagerly. "I'll distract Jack Frost and the goblins."

"How?" asked Kirsty.

"I'll use magic to put myself inside one of the presents that Jack Frost is opening," Holly replied. "That will give him a surprise!"

"That's a great idea," Rachel declared. "We'll creep around to the back of the sleigh. Then, while Holly creates a diversion, you grab the present, Kirsty. I'll try to drop the magic crown on Jack Frost's head."

"OK. Let's go," Kirsty whispered.

Holly nodded. She waved her wand above her head and immediately disappeared.

Rachel and Kirsty began to crawl on their hands and knees toward the sleigh, staying out of sight behind the rocks. Jack Frost was too busy unwrapping presents to notice them.

 And, luckily, the goblins were running backward and forward, trying to keep their grumpy master happy.

Their hearts thumping, the girls got closer and closer to the sleigh. The special present was so close now that Kirsty could reach out and touch it.

"Now we just wait for Holly to make her move," Rachel whispered.

The girls watched Jack Frost tear the paper off another present. "I'm bored," he grumbled. "Why can't I get a really nice present?" He threw the wrapping paper on the floor and held up a pretty wooden box. "I wonder what's inside?" he muttered.

Suddenly, the lid of
the box burst open.
Holly shot out in
a huge shower of
glittering red
holly berries and
fairy dust. Jack
Frost and the
goblins coughed
and spluttered in shock.

"This is our chance!" Kirsty cried,
while Jack Frost and his goblins stared at
Holly in surprise.

The Chase Is On!

Kirsty reached for the special present. Meanwhile, Rachel pulled the crown out of her pocket and stood up, ready to drop it onto Jack Frost's head.

"What's going on?" Jack Frost shouted, rubbing fairy dust out of his eyes. "It's that pesky Christmas Fairy, isn't it? Grab her!"

Kirsty had her hands on the present now, and Rachel was leaning over the sleigh with the crown. But just then, one of the goblins spotted her. "Look out!" he screeched, pointing a bony finger at Rachel.

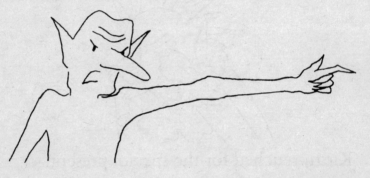

Jack Frost spun around. His cold, hard eyes met Rachel's, and she felt herself shiver. Quickly, Jack Frost waved his wand. The reindeer galloped off, pulling the sleigh behind them. Luckily, Kirsty was still hanging onto the ribbon that was tied around the special package.

As the sleigh moved away, the
present tumbled off and fell safely
into Kirsty's arms.

"I want you to catch that
fairy!" Jack Frost roared
at his goblin servants
as the reindeer
galloped toward
the tent
entrance,
taking the
sleigh with
them. "And
those girls, too!"

"Kirsty! Rachel!"
shouted Holly, who
was zooming up and
away from the goblins.
"You have to get out of here!"

The reindeer galloped out of the tent and flew up into the air. As the sleigh soared overhead, the shoppers looked up in amazement. They gasped, and then began clapping and cheering, thinking it was some sort of Christmas magic show.

The sleigh flew through the mall and out the big double doors. But back in the tent, the goblins were closing in on the girls, backing them into a corner. "We've got you now!" one of them snarled.

"You can't trick us and get away with it!" sneered another.

Kirsty and Rachel were very scared. "Split up and run for it when I give the word!" Rachel whispered. She waited until the goblins were close to them, and then shouted, "Now!"

Immediately, she and Kirsty ran as fast as they could in opposite directions. The goblins chased after them, but there was a lot of pushing and shoving and shouting. The clumsy goblins bumped into one another and tripped over their own big feet!

In the middle of the chaos, Rachel
and Kirsty both headed for the exit.
Kirsty reached it first. She noticed that
Rachel was nearly there, too, but a
goblin was very close behind her. As
Kirsty slipped out of the tent, she saw the
goblin reach for her friend!

The Great Escape

The goblin missed Rachel and fell over, tripping another goblin who was hot on his heels. The girls had escaped from the tent, but they knew that the goblins were right behind them. They didn't have much time to get away.

"Quick, Kirsty!" Rachel shouted.

"Those ropes that hold up the back of the tent — we need to pull them out!"

Kirsty knew exactly what Rachel had in mind. The two girls began pulling at the ropes with all their might.

Suddenly, there was a creaking sound as the ropes gave way. The large white tent wobbled and fell to the ground, trapping the goblins underneath the heavy canvas.

"We did it!" Kirsty gasped. "That was a great idea, Rachel!"

"Yes, but I think we'd better get out of here before those goblins escape," Rachel whispered. "It's almost time to meet Mom, anyway."

"Where's Holly?" asked Kirsty, looking around.

"Here I am!" called a tiny voice. Holly zoomed over to land on Kirsty's shoulder. All the shoppers were too busy staring at the collapsed tent to notice the tiny fairy.

"Are you all right?" Rachel asked anxiously.

"I'm fine!" Holly beamed. "Thank you for getting the second present. The Fairy King and Queen will be so happy!"

Kirsty held out the present, and Holly waved her wand over it. Fairy dust filled the air, and the present promptly vanished back to Fairyland.

"I almost got the crown on Jack Frost's head!" Rachel sighed as she dropped the crown carefully back into her pocket. "But he got away again. And we don't know where he went."

"Oh, yes, we do!" Holly told her excitedly. "While you were running from the goblins, I followed the sleigh and spoke to one of my reindeer friends."

"What did he say?" asked Rachel eagerly.

"He told me that Jack Frost is really annoyed that we keep finding him in the human world," Holly explained. "He

wants to open all of Santa's presents in
peace and quiet. So he told the reindeer
to take him to his ice castle right away."

"His ice castle!" Kirsty exclaimed.
"Where Jack Frost lives?"

Holly nodded.

"Do you know where it is, Holly?"
Rachel asked.

"Yes," Holly replied. "It's a cold, scary
place, but I can take you there
tomorrow, if you still want to help."

"Of course, we do!" said Kirsty and
Rachel together.

Holly beamed at them. "I'll head back to Fairyland now and report to King Oberon and Queen Titania," she went on. "Can you get me out of the mall?"

"Of course," Kirsty said, smiling. While Holly hid behind Kirsty's scarf, the girls walked quickly over to one of the doors. When nobody was looking, Holly slipped out

from behind the scarf, gave the girls a cheery wave, and zoomed up into the sky. The girls watched her fly away until she was out of sight.

Then they hurried back through the mall toward the glass elevators, where they had promised to meet Rachel's mom.

Mrs. Walker was already waiting for them, holding lots of shopping bags. "Hello, girls!" She smiled. "I thought you'd gotten lost! Did you both find everything you needed?"

"Almost!" Rachel replied with a quick glance at Kirsty.

"Did you see Santa's workshop?" Mrs. Walker went on, leading the way back to the car. "I heard it was beautiful — until the tent collapsed! But some of the parents were complaining that Santa was awfully grumpy."

Rachel and Kirsty grinned at each other. "He was!" Kirsty agreed.

"I wonder what's going to happen tomorrow, Rachel?" Kirsty whispered as Mrs. Walker unlocked the car. "Jack Frost's ice castle sounds scary."

"I know," Rachel whispered back. "But we can't let our fairy friends down."

"No, we can't," Kirsty said firmly. "We have to get Santa's sleigh and the third present."

"And this time, we'll get that magic crown on Jack Frost's head!" added Rachel. The girls exchanged a smile and climbed into the car. They were both very excited and a little bit nervous about what the next day might have in store!

Contents

Winter Wonderland

Rachel opened her eyes and yawned. She sat up in bed and looked over at Kirsty, who was still asleep. *It's Christmas Eve!* Rachel thought excitedly. But it would only be a merry Christmas if they managed to get the sleigh and all the presents back to Santa today. If they didn't, Jack Frost would ruin everything!

Rachel pushed back the blankets and shivered. Even though the heat was on, there was still a chill in the air. She went over to the window and looked outside. "Oh!" she gasped.

It had snowed heavily during the night, and the trees, grass, and shrubs were all hidden under a thick blanket of sparkling white snow.

"What is it?" Kirsty yawned.

"Sorry, did I wake you up?" asked Rachel. "I was just so surprised to see the snow!"

"Snow?" Kirsty gasped. She jumped out of bed and ran over to join Rachel. They both peered out of the frosty window.

"It looks like we're going to have a white Christmas." Rachel smiled.

"It'll be the best Christmas ever," Kirsty agreed. "As long as we make it back from Jack Frost's ice castle. . . ."

"Are you scared?" asked Rachel.

"A little," Kirsty replied. "But I'm not giving up. Are you?"

"No way!" Rachel laughed. "Come on. Let's get dressed and have breakfast. Then we can go outside."

The two girls hurried downstairs for

scrambled eggs and toast. Then they pulled on their coats and boots, and ran out into the yard. Their feet sank into the soft snow, leaving tracks all over the lawn. It started

snowing again, and pretty snowflakes
drifted down around them.

Kirsty rolled a snowball in her hands.
"Let's have a snowball
fight!" She grinned and
threw the snowball at
Rachel.

Laughing, Rachel
ducked. But before
the snowball reached
her, it exploded in the air
like fireworks. Tiny sparkling
red icicles shot in all directions. As Kirsty
and Rachel watched in amazement,
Holly burst out of the snowball.

"Here I am!" she cried, shaking
snowflakes from her red dress. "Are you
ready, girls? It's time to go to Jack Frost's
ice castle!"

The Ice Castle

"We're ready!" Rachel said bravely.

Kirsty nodded and checked her coat pocket to make sure she had the magic crown.

Then Holly waved her wand in the air. Berry-red fairy dust drifted down over the girls, and they began to shrink. In a moment, they were fairy-size and had thin wings on their backs.

Holly fluttered up into the air, and Rachel and Kirsty followed her.

"Here we go!" Holly said, waving her wand again.

It was snowing heavily now, and the falling snowflakes began to spin and

dance around the girls until Rachel and
Kirsty couldn't see anything at all.

Then, the blizzard of snow cleared as
quickly as it had begun. Rachel
and Kirsty gasped. They
weren't in the Walkers'
backyard anymore!
Instead, they were
sitting in a tree,
staring at Jack
Frost's ice castle.

The castle stood
on a tall hill
under a gloomy,
gray winter sky. It
was built out of sheets
of ice. It had five towers
tipped with icy blue
peaks. The ice glittered

and sparkled like diamonds, but the palace still looked cold and scary.

"Be careful," Holly whispered as a few goblins walked underneath the tree. "There are goblins everywhere. We'll never get in through the main gate."

"Maybe we can find a way in from above," Rachel suggested, looking upward.

"Good idea," Holly replied. "Follow me!" The girls trailed Holly as she flew up toward one of the ice-blue towers. "See what I mean?" Holly said quietly. Rachel and Holly peered down at the castle below.

Holly was right. There were goblin guards at every door!

"Maybe we can find an open window," whispered Rachel.

Holly nodded. "Let's split up and take a look.  We'll meet back here in a few minutes." They all flew off in different directions. Kirsty went to look around the tops of the towers, one by one. There were lots of windows, but all of them were

locked. She flew back to meet Rachel and Holly.

Rachel was already waiting. "I didn't have any luck." She sighed. "Did you?"

Kirsty shook her head sadly.

At that moment, Holly fluttered down to join them.

"Did you get lost?" asked Kirsty.

"I had to hide from one of the goblins," Holly explained. "He was on guard duty, and he almost spotted me!"

"We didn't find any open windows,"
Rachel told her. "Did you?"

Holly shook her head. "No, but I
found another way in!" She grinned.
"Follow me."

Holly led the girls
to the roof of
the castle and
pointed down.
"Look!" she
said. "A trap
door!" Kirsty
gasped.

"When I was
hiding from the goblin,
I saw him lift the trap
door and go into the
castle," Holly told the girls. "And I don't
think he locked it on the other side."

They checked to make sure that there were no goblins around, then flew down to the trap door. It was a slab of ice with a steel ring on the top.

"It looks very heavy," Rachel said with a frown.

"That's no problem," Holly said, smiling. She waved her wand and the trap door suddenly flew open in a whirl of fairy dust.

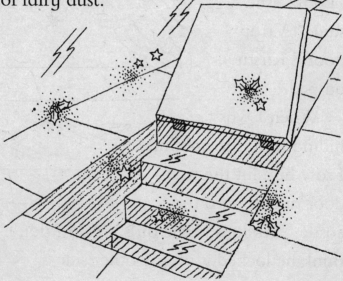

Below were steps of ice, which led down into the castle. Shivering, Rachel, Kirsty, and Holly flew inside.

"We have to start looking for Santa's sleigh right away," Holly whispered to the girls.

"It's not easy to hide a sleigh and eight reindeer!" said Rachel.

"Maybe they're in the stables?" Kirsty suggested.

"That's a good place to start," said Holly. "But keep a sharp lookout for goblins!"

The friends flew down the winding
staircase toward the ground floor of the
castle. But as they fluttered around a
corner, they bumped right into a goblin
who was on his way up the stairs.

"Fairies!" the goblin roared. "What are
you doing here?" He tried to grab at
Holly, but she darted out of reach.
"Help! Fairies!"

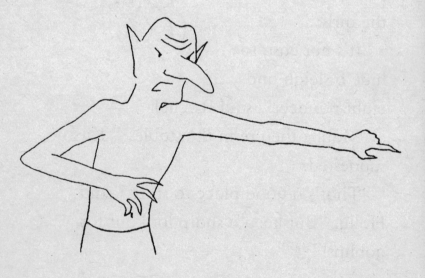

Holly, Rachel, and Kirsty turned and flew back up the stairs. But as they reached the next corner, they heard the loud clatter of footsteps. Six more goblins were rushing toward them!

Caught!

The three friends tried to dodge out
of the way, but they were completely
surrounded by goblins. Holly and Rachel
were both caught right away. Kirsty tried
to fly overhead, but one goblin jumped
onto another one's shoulders and grabbed
hold of her ankle.

The goblins laughed gleefully. "Now

you're our prisoners!" they cried. "Jack Frost is going to be so happy with us!"

The goblins took their prisoners through the ice castle and into the Great Hall. It was a huge room carved from shining sheets of ice. At one end was Jack Frost's throne. It was made of glittering icicles that had been twisted into shape.

But Jack Frost wasn't sitting on his throne. He was in Santa's sleigh! The reindeer were still harnessed to it, and they were munching on bales of hay. Jack Frost was unwrapping more presents, and the floor was covered with wrapping paper and ribbons.

Rachel, Holly, and Kirsty trembled as

the goblins pushed them toward Jack
Frost.

"Look what we brought you!" one of
the goblins called triumphantly.

Jack Frost looked up at the girls. "You
again!" he snarled, staring at them with
cold, hard eyes. "You're always trying to
ruin my fun!"

He shook his fist.
Rachel gasped as she
spotted the present
that Jack Frost held
in his other hand. He
hadn't opened it yet.
It was still wrapped
in pretty gold paper
and tied with a
rainbow-colored
bow. It was the third

special present that King Oberon and
Queen Titania had asked the girls to find!

Rachel glanced at Kirsty and Holly.
They'd spotted the present, too! But how
were they going to keep Jack Frost from
opening it?

Kirsty was thinking the same thing as
Rachel. She stared down at
the piles of wrapping paper
on the floor, and suddenly,
she had an idea.

"What am I going
to do with you?"
Jack Frost was
muttering,
tapping his long,
thin fingers on
top of the present.
"I think I'll put you

in my deepest ice dungeon and leave you there for one hundred years!"

"Rachel," Kirsty whispered. "I have an idea. Can you distract the goblins and Jack Frost for a few minutes?"

Rachel looked at her friend curiously, then nodded. "OK," she whispered back.

"Should we take them to the dungeons, Master?" asked one of the goblins.

"I haven't decided yet!" Jack Frost snapped. "Now be quiet while I open this present." He lifted the package and shook it. "I can't wait to see what's inside!"

The goblins moved forward, eager to see what was inside the package, too. The goblin who was holding on to Rachel loosened his grip slightly, and Rachel saw her chance. She zoomed up into the air, then flew straight for the door.

"Get her!" Jack Frost yelled furiously.

The goblins rushed after Rachel, shouting and tripping

over one another's feet. At the same time,
Kirsty bent down and grabbed a piece
of silver wrapping paper and a purple
ribbon from the floor. While Jack Frost
watched the goblins from the sleigh,
Kirsty pulled the gold bag with the magic
crown in it out of her pocket. She quickly
wrapped it in the silver paper and tied
the ribbon around the package. Holly
gave her a puzzled look. She had no idea
what Kirsty was up to!

Jack Frost was getting more and more angry as his goblins tried to catch Rachel. Eventually, he waved his wand, and Rachel's wings instantly froze in midair. She fell to the ground, landing on top of two goblins.

"Now," Jack Frost snapped as two more goblins dragged Rachel to her feet, "I'm going to open this present!"

"Please, Your Majesty," said Kirsty, stepping forward. "May I say something?"

Jack Frost glared at her. "Make it quick!" he said.

"Won't you take pity on us?" asked Kirsty. "We only came here to get this one very special present." She held up the crown, wrapped in silver paper. "It's for the Fairy King, and it's very important. Please let us take it to him!"

Jack Frost's beady eyes lit up as he stared at the present in Kirsty's hands. "A present for King Oberon?" he muttered. "Give it to me!"

"But —" Kirsty began.

"Now!" Jack Frost roared.

A goblin pushed Kirsty forward. Jack Frost dropped the present he was holding and snatched the other one from Kirsty's hands.

Kirsty tried not to smile. She knew Jack Frost would take the Fairy King's present for himself! Now he was ripping the ribbon and paper away to reveal the golden bag. He put his hand inside and drew out the glittering crown.

"A-ha!" he declared triumphantly. "It's a new crown!" He lifted the crown and lowered it onto his frosty white hair.

Immediately, Jack Frost vanished!

A Magical Journey

The goblins gasped in surprise. They didn't know what had happened to their master. Would they be next? They ran around the Great Hall in panic. Some tried to hide under the piles of wrapping paper, while others huddled behind giant icicles.

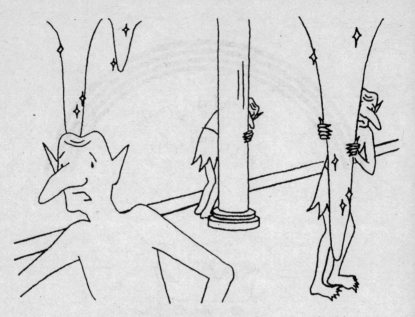

"Great idea, Kirsty!" Holly laughed.

"Jack Frost has been sent to the Fairy
King and Queen," cried Rachel. She
jumped into the magic sleigh and picked
up the third present. "And it's time for us
to leave, too!"

"But how are we going to get out of
the castle?" asked Kirsty as she hopped
into the sleigh.

"Don't worry about that," Holly said cheerfully. "The sleigh is magical, you know!" She patted one of the reindeer on the head. "Take us back to Santa, please, my friends!"

The reindeer tossed their antlers joyfully and began to gallop off across the Great Hall. Goblins jumped out of the way as the sleigh picked up speed. Then it rose into the air, heading for the icy roof.

"Oh!" gasped Rachel. "We're going to crash!"

But, magically, the ice melted away as  the sleigh approached. Soon, the girls were soaring out of the castle and up into the clouds. Then the reindeer raced across the sky so fast that everything was a blur.

"Here's Santa's workshop!" Holly called at last.

The reindeer slowed down, and the sleigh floated toward the ground. Rachel and Kirsty peered out eagerly. Below them, they saw the pretty log cabin that they remembered from the fairy pool. And there was a big crowd of elves outside, dancing in the snow. The bells on their hats tinkled merrily.

"Hooray!" they cried happily. "You found the sleigh and the reindeer!" As the sleigh landed, the elves ran over to pet the reindeer and feed them carrots.

Rachel and Kirsty gasped as Santa himself came running out of the cabin. He was in such a hurry that he hadn't even buttoned up his red coat! "Welcome! Welcome!"

Santa called, beaming. "My beautiful sleigh and my precious reindeer are safe, thanks to you!"

"Are we in time to save Christmas, Santa?" Rachel asked anxiously.

Santa nodded. "Oh, yes." He smiled. "It's going to be a wonderful Christmas!"

"But what about the presents Jack Frost already opened?" Kirsty wanted to know. "Does that mean some children won't get anything?"

"Oh, no!" Santa said, looking shocked. "That would never do! My elves have made plenty of extra presents."

As he spoke, a group of elves ran out of the cabin, carrying armfuls of brightly colored gifts. They piled them up in the magic sleigh.

Santa turned to the three girls when the sleigh was full of presents again. "The king and queen will want to see you.

Come with me. I'll drop you off on my way to deliver these gifts."

Rachel and Kirsty climbed back into the sleigh. They couldn't believe it. They were going to ride with Santa Claus on Christmas Eve!

Holly joined them as Santa grabbed the reins. "Let's go, my friends!" Santa

called happily to the reindeer. "We have a lot of work to do today!"

Rachel and Kirsty grinned at each other as the sleigh rose into the sky again. They were off to Fairyland!

A Fairy Merry Christmas

As Santa's sleigh got closer to Fairyland, the girls and Holly could see sparkling fireworks exploding below them. The sound of music and fairy laughter drifted up to the sleigh.

"There's a big party at the palace." Holly smiled. "They must have heard the good news!"

The reindeer flew lower, and there was a shout from the fairies below as they spotted the sleigh. Rachel and Kirsty waved as they saw all their old friends waiting for them.

"Wonderful job!" called King Oberon as the sleigh landed.

"You helped Holly save Christmas!" Queen Titania added.

The fairies cheered as Rachel, Kirsty, and Holly stepped out of the sleigh.

"We brought you this," Rachel said, handing the third special present to King Oberon.

"Thank you!" The king beamed. "Will you stay and join the party, Santa?"

Santa shook his head. "I'd love to, but I have a lot of

work to do!" He laughed and shook the reins. "Merry Christmas!"

"Merry Christmas!" everyone called as the silver sleigh flew out of sight.

"What happened to Jack Frost?" asked Rachel.

The king frowned. "His magic powers have been taken away from him," he explained.

"And he must stay in his ice castle for a whole year before he is allowed to use magic again!" the queen said. "But now it's time to celebrate Christmas. We have special gifts for all three of you."

She clapped her hands, and two small fairies hurried forward. They carried the two special presents that Holly had brought back to Fairyland earlier.

"These presents are so special because they are for the three of you!" the queen said.

Rachel, Holly, and Kirsty gasped in surprise, and everyone laughed.

"Since it's Christmas Eve, you can open them right away." The king smiled and handed Holly the present that Rachel had just given him.

Eagerly, Holly tore the gold paper off the package and peeked inside the box.

"A new wand!" she cried. "It's beautiful!"

"It is extra powerful," Queen Titania told her as Holly twirled the wand above her head. It left a trail of magic sparkles

behind it and made the sweet sound of tinkling Christmas bells. "It will help you make Christmas more magical than ever before." The queen smiled.

"Thank you!" Holly beamed.

Queen Titania handed the other two presents to Rachel and Kirsty. They couldn't wait to see what was inside! Rachel managed to open hers a second before Kirsty, and she gasped with delight.

"It's a fairy doll!" Rachel said, her eyes shining. "Look, Kirsty — a fairy for the top of your Christmas tree!"

The doll sparkled with magic. She wore a white dress that glittered with silver and gold, and had a sparkling crown over her long hair. Kirsty had a doll that was exactly the same.

"I can't wait to get home and put it on our Christmas tree!" Kirsty said, smiling happily.

"There's just one more thing!" The queen laughed. "These dolls are magical. Every year, they will bring you a special Christmas present from the fairies!"

Rachel and Kirsty were thrilled. They'd never expected this!

"But we shouldn't keep you any longer," the king said suddenly. "It's time for you to go home, or you'll be late for Christmas!"

Quickly, the girls said their good-byes. They both gave Holly a hug, and

then the queen
waved her wand.
"Thank you!"
she called.
"And Merry
Christmas!"

"Merry
Christmas!"
Rachel and
Kirsty replied as
they were caught
up in a whirl of
magic fairy dust.

"Merry Christmas!" called all
the fairies.

Suddenly, the fairy voices died away,
the magic dust cleared, and Rachel and
Kirsty found themselves back to their
normal size in the Walkers' yard.

"We did it, Rachel!" Kirsty laughed breathlessly. "We saved Christmas!"

"Let's go in the house and put my fairy doll on top of the Christmas tree," Rachel grinned.

The girls ran inside. Kirsty watched as Rachel placed the fairy doll carefully on the top of the tree.

"She looks beautiful!" Rachel said happily.

Just then, the doorbell rang. Rachel ran to see who it was and found Kirsty's mom and dad standing outside.

"Merry Christmas!" said Mr. and Mrs. Tate with a smile.

"Mom! Dad!" Kirsty cried, rushing over to them.

Mr. and Mrs. Tate stayed for hot chocolate and pie, and then it was time for Kirsty to leave. She gave Rachel a big hug.

"Have a great Christmas!" Kirsty told her friend.

"You, too," Rachel replied. Then she stood on the doorstep with her mom and dad, waving at the Tates as they drove away.

Mr. and Mrs. Walker closed the front door and returned to the cozy living room, but Rachel stayed in the hall with Buttons. She stared up at the glittering fairy on top of the tree.

Then Rachel blinked hard. Was she seeing things? The fairy had smiled at her, and a cloud of magic sparkles had drifted from her wand!

Rachel looked down to see where the sparkles had fallen — and there was a present under the tree that hadn't been there before. It was wrapped in gold paper and tied with a bow that glittered in all the colors of the rainbow.

Rachel smiled and patted Buttons. This really was going to be the best Christmas ever!

RAINBOW
magic™
SPECIAL EDITION

Rachel and Kirsty helped Holly save the
Christmas magic, but Jack Frost is up to
his old tricks!
Can the girls help keep the holidays merry
and bright?

Enjoy this peek at

Stella

the Star Fairy!

Darkness Falls

Mrs. Tate popped her head around
the door. "Are you ready, girls?" she
asked. "It's time to leave for the
Christmas Fair."

"Coming, Mom," Kirsty said,
jumping up.

"I'm really glad I could come and
visit," said Rachel Walker, as she

followed her best friend into the hall to get their coats. Rachel was visiting over Christmas break. Her parents were picking her up on Christmas Eve.

"Me, too," Kirsty replied. "You're going to love the fair. And who knows . . . we might even see a Christmas fairy!"

"I forgot to tell you!" Kirsty said, pulling on her boots. "Every year, someone from my school is chosen to be the fair's Christmas King or Queen. This year, it's my friend Molly."

"Wow! I bet she's really excited," said Rachel, smiling.

Kirsty nodded as her parents joined them.

"Everybody ready?" Mrs. Tate said. "Then let's go!"

Even though it was a cold, frosty night, the square was packed with people! They bustled around stalls selling brightly-painted tree decorations, Christmas cookies, hot chocolate, and gifts.

"Isn't it great?" Kirsty said, her eyes shining. She pointed at a raised platform in the middle of the square. The mayor of Wetherbury was standing there next to a large switch. "It'll be even better when the Christmas Queen turns on the lights," Kirsty added.

Rachel glanced around. She could see dark shapes made out of unlit lightbulbs above their heads, but it was hard to figure out what the shapes were. She was looking forward to seeing them all lit up.

The mayor helped Molly up the steps as the crowd clapped.

"I would like to wish everyone in Wetherbury a very merry Christmas!" Molly announced. Then she pulled the light switch with a flourish.

The square lit up in a blaze of color as the lightbulbs sprang to life. Everyone *ooh*ed and *aah*ed as they gazed around.

There were hundreds of snowflakes in different sizes strung on wires overhead, and they all glittered with rainbow-colored lights.

"These are definitely the best lights Wetherbury has ever had!" Kirsty said.

But just then, one of the snowflakes above their heads began to flicker. As the girls glanced upward, every single one of the beautiful snowflake lights suddenly went out!

RAINBOW magic™

There's Magic in Every Series!

The Rainbow Fairies

The Weather Fairies

The Jewel Fairies

The Pet Fairies

The Fun Day Fairies

The Petal Fairies

The Dance Fairies

The Music Fairies

The Sports Fairies

The Party Fairies

Read them all!

■ SCHOLASTIC

www.scholastic.com

www.rainbowmagiconline.com

RMFAIRY2